Think & Play the Social Scouts Way™:

FIREFIGHTER LEO TO THE RESCUE !

by

Amy Wilhelm, M.S., CCC-SLP

Heather Marenda-Miller, M.S., CCC-SLP

Illustrated by Alen Haljevac

THINK & PLAY THE SOCIAL SCOUTS WAY: FIREFIGHTER LEO TO THE RESCUE!

By Amy Wilhelm, M.S., CCC-SLP and Heather Marenda-Miller, M.S., CCC-SLP

Illustrated by Alen Haljevac

Published by Social Scouts, LLC

3637 Motor Avenue, Suite 280, Los Angeles, CA 90034

www.socialscoutsla.com

ISBN 9781635351163

Library of Congress Control Number: 2017908402

This book is intended to be read to or with children from ages 3 to 7 and was designed to enhance social development and increase speech and language skills, as well as heighten imagination through play.

Book design and cover design by Alen Haljevac

Printed in the U.S.A.

Dedication:

To all the children we have worked with over the years.
You motivated us every day to become better therapists and
continually inspired us with all of your accomplishments.
You have been our best teachers.

Acknowledgments:

A big thank you to Lewie Miller for letting us turn the living room into our
"writing office" on Saturdays. We also thank our families, friends and colleagues
who have supported us, provided insight and encouraged us along our journey.
We are forever indebted to our illustrator, Alen Haljevac, for understanding our
vision and bringing it to life more beautifully than we could have imagined.
To Nancy Sayles for her guidance and expertise in publishing and press and
enlightening us with humor along the way.

Leo wants to play firefighter, but he's not sure what to do. So he wonders,

"HOW DO I PRETEND TO BE A FIREFIGHTER?"

BEFORE Leo can play firefighter, he needs to think about everything he knows about firefighters.

A firefighter is a man or woman who works in the community. Firefighters help when there are emergencies. The firefighter's job is to put out fires. Firefighters also rescue people and pets. The firefighter drives a fire engine from the fire station to the fire or place of emergency.

He thinks, "**WHAT DOES A FIREFIGHTER WEAR?**"

oxygen mask

oxygen tank

fire jacket

fire gloves

fire helmet

fire boots

A firefighter wears special firefighting gear to an emergency.

fire pants

Leo wonders, **"WHERE DOES A FIREFIGHTER WORK?"**

Firefighters work at the fire station and different places all around the community.

Can you tell where each firefighter is working in the community?

He thinks, "**WHAT** **EQUIPMENT DOES A**

axe

walkie-talkies

oxygen mask

megaphone

hose

fire hydrant

FIREFIGHTER USE FOR AN EMERGENCY?"

fire extinguisher

water

ladder

fire engine

What does the firefighter do with each of these objects?

Leo thinks, **"WHAT DOES A FIREFIGHTER DO AT THE FIRE STATION?"**

Look at the pictures and describe what each firefighter is doing at the fire station.

He thinks, "**WHAT DOES A FIREFIGHTER DO IN THE COMMUNITY?**"

Look at the pictures and describe what each firefighter is doing in the community.

Leo wonders, "WHAT DOES A FIREFIGHTER SAY AT THE FIRE STATION?"

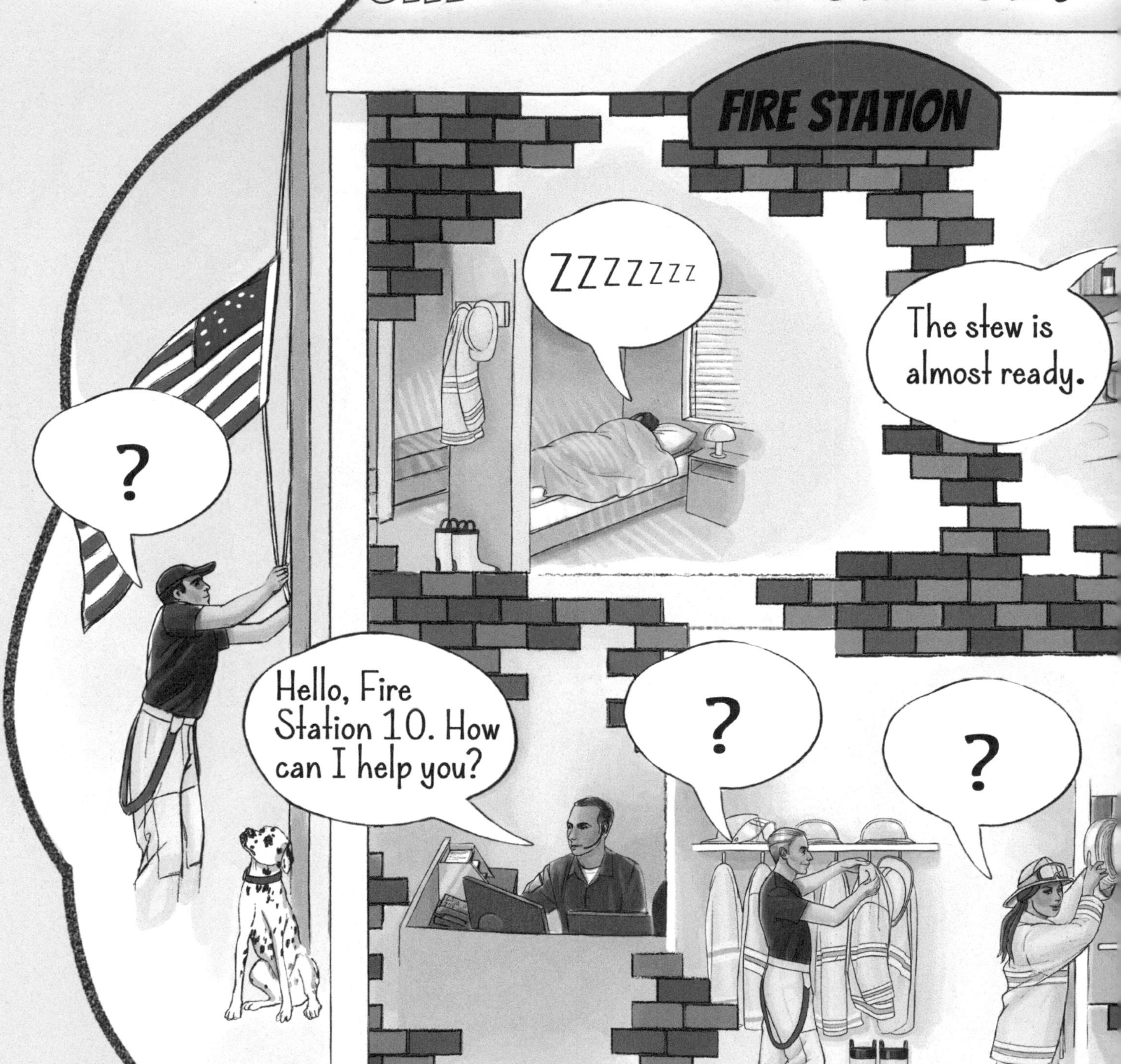

Find all of the speech bubbles with a question mark.
What do you think the firefighter is saying?

He wonders, **"WHAT DOES A FIREFIGHTER SAY IN THE COMMUNITY?"**

Find all of the speech bubbles with a question mark.
What do you think the firefighter is saying?

AFTER Leo thinks about all the things he knows about firefighters, he feels excited to play! Now Leo can imagine himself being a firefighter.

Leo gets ready to play firefighter. He gets all the things he needs and sets up his fire station. Today Leo's idea is to put out a fire at a burning building and rescue the people inside.

FIRST, Leo rings the fire alarm and puts on his firefighter gear.

DING! DING! DING!

NEXT, he climbs into his fire truck and drives to the emergency.

THEN, Leo sprays water on the fire with his hose.

AFTER he puts out the fire, Leo rescues his toy cow.

LAST, Leo drives back to the fire station and cleans up all of his firefighter toys.

Leo had so much fun playing firefighter, he's wondering about what the emergency will be next time he plays!

Do you have any ideas about how Firefighter Leo will save the day next time?

HEY GROWN-UPS!

Now your child is ready to play firefighter just like Leo!

The sequence cards on the next page are intended to be cut apart and used during playtime in either a left-to-right or an up-and-down order to assist your child in following the steps and completing a full circle of play called a play plan. The sequence cards are categorized by color and a corresponding shape on the back to indicate the 3 important parts of play.

LET'S PLAN

Every set of sequence pictures begins with 1 yellow card — the **LET'S PLAN** card teaches the importance of gathering items and getting ready to play. Encourage your child to think of the items the firefighter wears and uses, and the places he/she works. This is the time to have your child help with:

- gathering the related toys (if you don't have toys specific to firefighters, think of items you could use to substitute during play)
- gathering dress-up clothes
- choosing or setting up a location for play
- choosing a stuffed animal/figurine to use in play

LET'S PLAY

Every set of sequence pictures contains 4 green cards — the **LET'S PLAY** cards teach how to play in a simple, easy-to-follow order just as Leo did in the story. Have your child talk about the items and/or actions in the picture on each green card before beginning play, taking time to discuss:

- the items Leo is using, both real and pretend (e.g. real - fire helmet, pretend - jump rope for hose)
- the actions Leo is performing in each picture
- the clothes Leo is wearing
- Leo's facial expressions and body language

Prior to playing, mimic each action paired with a sound effect and/or language, as appropriate, for each of the 4 play steps. Encourage your child to put the 4 pictures in the correct order and ask him/her, "What happens next?" throughout. Encourage your child to explain the sequence emphasizing the concepts of **FIRST, NEXT, THEN, AFTER.**

LET'S PUT IT AWAY

Every set of sequence pictures ends with 1 red card — the **LET'S PUT IT AWAY** card teaches the importance of cleaning up and completing the play plan. Emphasize the concept **LAST.**

Your child should help clean up and put toys back where they belong, promoting good manners and organizational skills.

For information about additional activities, visit www.SocialScoutsLA.com

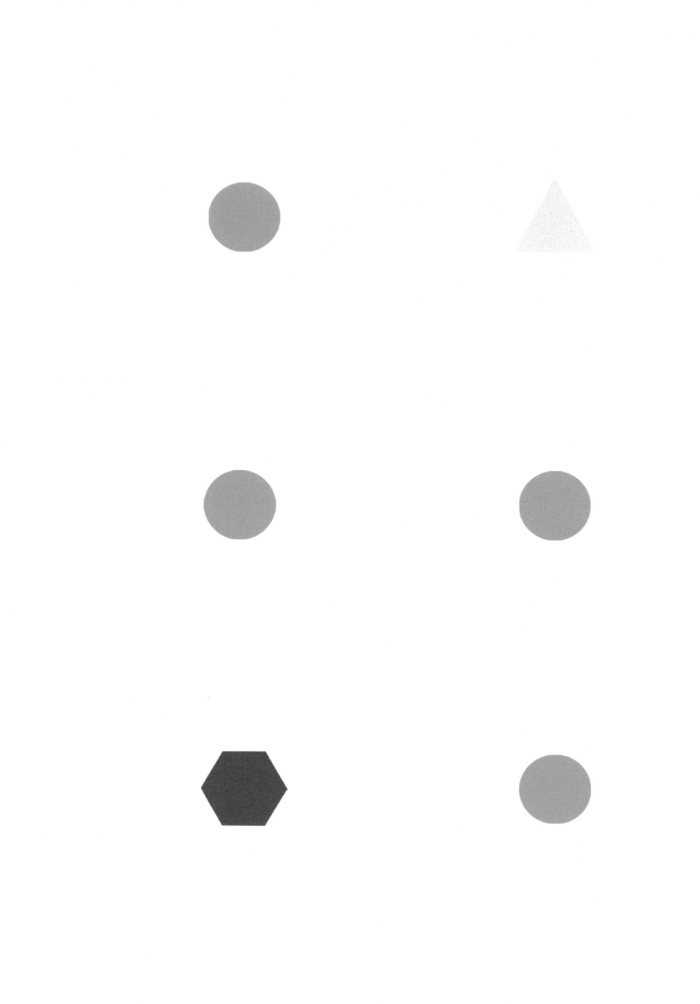

CPSIA information can be obtained
at www.ICGtesting.com
Printed in the USA
BVOW05s1138291117
501547BV00025B/1344/P

9 781635 351163